CALOR

A Story of Warmth for All Ages

Text by Juanita Alba

Illustrations by Amado M. Peña, Jr.

LECTORUM
PUBLICATIONS, INC.
557 BROADWAY NEW YORK, NY 10012-3919

Abuelito decía que el calor del sol es la cobija de los pobres.

My grandfather used to say that the warmth of the sun is the blanket of the poor.

COLCHA SERIES: LA PROMESA

**El calor siempre ha sido mi amigo.
Siempre lo he querido.**

*The warmth has always been my friend.
I have always loved it.*

LA CENTINELA

El calor de mi mamá me da fuerza porque sé que su amor siempre está conmigo. Haga bien o no, ella siempre me quiere.

My mother's warmth gives me strength because I know that her love is always with me. Whether I do well or not, she always loves me.

LOS CUENTOS

Yo sé que el calor vive entre lo anaranjado y lo colorado.

I know that warmth lives between the shades of orange and red.

DANZA DE COLORES

**El calor de mi abuelita me hace
que me acurruque con ella.
Su calor tiene el olor a rosas frescas y
tortillas recién hechas.**

*My grandmother's warmth makes me feel
like cuddling up to her. Her warmth
has the smell of fresh roses and
freshly made tortillas.*

ABUELITA: LA CUENTISTA

11

**Todo lo que mamá hace – las colchas,
el chile guisado, sus caricias –
demuestra el calor que vive en ella.**

*Everything that Mother does – making quilts,
cooking chili, her caresses –
shows the warmth that lives in her.*

13

COLCHA SERIES: LA TEJEDORA

**Mis tíos son muchos. Nada se compara
con el poder de ese calor.**

*I have many uncles. Nothing compares to
the power of their warmth.*

DANZA DEL BISONTE

**También los animales buscan
el calor del amor.**

*The animals also look for
the warmth of love.*

PATRONES

**Yo sé que cuando la gente baila, siente calor.
Sus caras se ponen
rojas y llenas de sudor.**

*I know that when people dance,
warmth covers them. Their faces turn
red and sweaty.*

DANZA DE LOS ARTESANOS

**Cuando pasa el frío, llega el calor,
y todos le damos la bienvenida.**

*After winter has passed,
the warmth arrives and everybody welcomes it.*

EL SÁBADO, DÍA DEL MERCADO

**El calor es bueno para hacer panecitos
y merendar con chocolate caliente.**

*Warmth is good for baking bread and
serving with hot chocolate.*

HACIENDO PAN

**No hay nada mejor que ver tu casa
a lo lejos y saber que pronto llegarás al
calor de tu familia que te quiere.**

*There's nothing better than to see
your house at a distance and to know that
soon you will reach the warmth of
the family that loves you.*

COMING HOME

**Con un regalo,
viene el calor del amor.**

*With a gift,
comes the warmth of love.*

LOS REGALOS

**Papá dice que mestizo soy,
indio y español.
Por los dos lados, mi tierra
conoce el calor.**

*My father says that I am Mestizo,
Indian and Spanish.
From both sides, my heritage
knows warmth.*

ARTESANAS DE TAOS

Cuando me pongo a pensar,
sé que el calor en mi corazón
es el amor que siento por todos
aquellos que han llenado mi vida de felicidad.

When I pause to think,
I know that the warmth in my heart
is the love I feel for everyone
who has filled my life with happiness.

AUTORETRATO

<u>Dedication</u>

Este libro está dedicado a Luz y Lupe,
dos hermanas, que nos criaron con el calor de la familia.

This book is dedicated to Luz and Lupe,
two sister, who brought us up with the warmth of family.

Text copyright © 1995 by Juanita Alba
Art copyright © 1995 by Amado M. Peña, Jr.

First published in the United States of America in 1995 by WRS Publishing.
This edition published by
Lectorum Publications, Inc.
557 Broadway, New York, NY 10012
Under license from WRS.
Book design by Kenneth Turbeville.
Jacket design by Joe James.

1-930332-62-9 (PB)
1-880507-26-9 (HC)

Printed in China.

10 9 8 7 6 5 4

Library of Congress Cataloging-in-Publication Data
Alba, Juanita
Calor: a story of warmth for all ages / text by Juanita Alba;
illustrations by Amado M. Peña, Jr.
p.   cm.
English and Spanish
I. Peña, Amado Maurilio, 1943-   II. Title.
P273.A48   1995   94-26332
CIP
AC